W9-CPE-047

The Dump Man's Treasures

In memory of
Uncle Clayton (Ambrose), who loved to
find treasures and who *was* a treasure —LP

For Janet, in memory of dump-picking days —MBO

Typography by the Roxmont Group.

Printed in China / OGP
2 4 5 3 1

Down East
www.downeast.com
Distributed to the trade by National Book Network

LIBRARY OF CONGRESS CATALOGING-IN-PUBLICATION DATA

Plourde, Lynn.

The dump man's treasures / by Lynn Plourde ; illustrated by Mary Beth Owens.

p. cm.

Summary: As people continually throw their books away, the dump man restores and re-circulates them, which pleases only the children, but one day when the dump does not open, only the children know where to possibly find the dump man.

ISBN-13: 978-0-89272-725-4 (trade hardcover : alk. paper)

[1. Refuse and refuse disposal--Fiction. 2. Books--Fiction. 3. Libraries--Fiction.] I. Owens, Mary Beth, ill. II. Title.

PZ7.P724Du 2008

[E]--dc22

2007044890

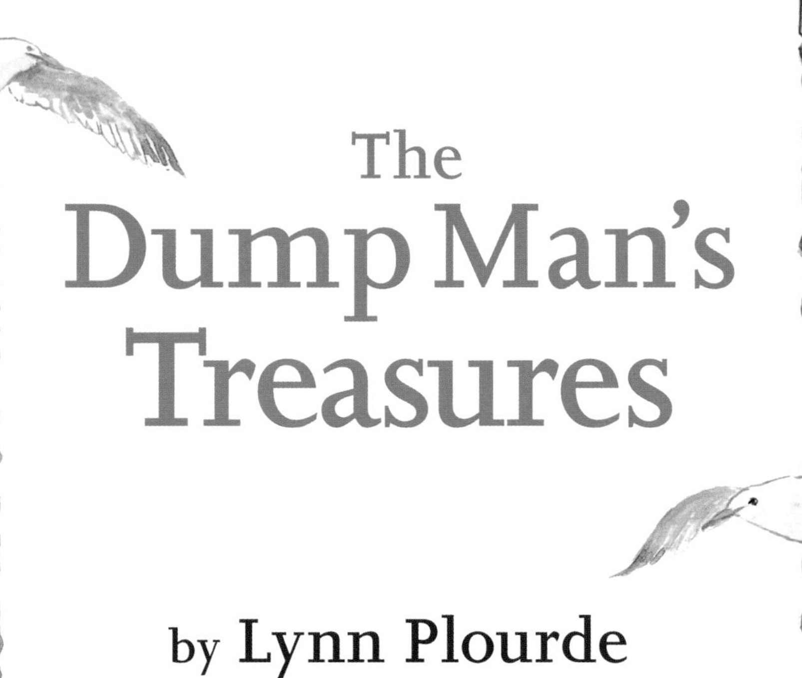

The Dump Man's Treasures

by Lynn Plourde

illustrated by Mary Beth Owens

Down East

Back when dumps were called dumps, not landfills or recycling centers, way up in the northeast corner of the United States, in the small village of Shiretown, Maine, Mr. Pottle was the dump man.

He certainly would answer if someone called him by his real names, Bill or Mr. Pottle. But most folks just called him the dump man. He didn't mind. That was his job, and he loved it.

And, oh, the treasures he'd find!

Like the rocker missing a few spindles, but Mr. Pottle fit in that chair like a baby in a cradle. There was no better throne for watching over his dump.

Or the wobbly globe. Mr. Pottle would spin it with his eyes closed and his finger out. Wherever it stopped, he'd imagine visiting hot spots near the equator or cold places near the poles. Didn't cost him a penny—just a little imagination.

Or the weathervane. Mr. Pottle didn't have a clue why someone would throw away a perfectly good one just because of a little rust. It still gave a creaky whirl in the wind. With that weathervane plus some cloud-watching, Mr. Pottle knew for certain when a storm was a-brewing, so no one had to unload trash in the rain.

But best of all were the books.

The dump man wouldn't let anyone throw away a single book.

Mr. Pottle offered to fix books. He taped torn pages, glued bindings back on, and set books by the simmering potpourri on his hotplate to hide their musty smells.

But still people threw away books.

Mr. Pottle waggled his finger. "Shame, shame! Books are treasures. You don't throw away treasures!"

The children of Shiretown agreed. They wanted to keep every book they'd ever owned—even their baby books.

But some parents wouldn't hear of such a thing: "You've

outgrown these." "We don't have any more room for books." "You've already read them a hundred times."

So they still threw away books.

Since Mr. Pottle couldn't stop people from discarding books, he started his own library—the dump library.

He built shelves out of mismatched pieces of pine, oak, and maple that he salvaged from discarded tables, beds, and bureaus.

He arranged a hodgepodge of books on a mishmash of shelves. Cookbooks with kids' books. Science with science fiction. Histories with mysteries.

Then anyone who came to the dump could just dig through the books and borrow whatever they wanted and return them on their next dump visit. No signing them out. No late fees. People could even keep the books they liked or give them away as gifts. Mr. Pottle only had one rule—NO THROWING BOOKS AWAY.

Some grown-ups in Shiretown were a little concerned about the dump library. "What if it keeps people away from the *town* library?" they asked.

"There should be more rules."

"What if someone catches a disease from those books that have been near all that garbage?"

The kids said, “Who cares?” They all begged to go with their parents on dump day to check out the “new” old books Mr. Pottle had saved since last week.

But there were more grown-ups than kids in Shiretown, and still people threw away books. Soon Mr. Pottle didn't have any more room on the shelves in his shack. Since he wouldn't throw away a single book, the dump man needed a new plan.

Early in the morning before the dump opened, or late in the afternoon after the dump closed, Mr. Pottle filled a wobbly old grocery cart with books and headed to town. He wheeled that cart everywhere—to nursing homes, to back-alley apartments, even along the riverbank where the homeless folks slept. Each day he gave away books, books, and more books.

The grown-ups said, "The dump man has gone mad. Now he's taking his trashy books all over town."

The kids giggled. "What fun!" they shouted as they followed him on their bicycles after school.

But early one Saturday morning, on the busiest dump day of the week, Mr. Pottle was nowhere to be found.

Cars and trucks were backed up at the gate. Horns blared and tempers flared.

"Open the gate!"

"We don't have all day!"

"Hurry up!"

"You're making us late for our other errands!"

As the grown-ups shook their heads and honked their horns, the kids huddled and hatched a plan.

"Something's wrong."

"Mr. Pottle's never late."

"We've gotta find him."

"Hurry home, everyone. Grab your bikes and search *everywhere*."

The kids raced all over town.

They checked the dump man's house. But no one answered their knocks, and the only movement they could see through the windows was his cat pacing back and forth on the rug by the front door.

They looked behind the piles at the dump. Mounds of twisted metal, hunks of wood, and chunks of glass, but no sign of Mr. Pottle.

They searched all the back roads around town, listening for the faintest of sounds and watching for the tiniest of movements.

There he was!

A wheel to his grocery cart had fallen off, causing it to tip over and crash into a deep ditch. Mr. Pottle had broken his ankle, but that didn't stop him from crawling on his hands and knees, trying to collect all the books that had toppled in with him.

As the kids waited with him for the ambulance to arrive, he thanked them for coming to his rescue. They told him not to worry as they set to work rescuing his books.

Later that day, word spread around Shiretown that Mr. Pottle had to have surgery on his ankle and was under doctor's orders to stay home until it healed.

After spending a few days in the hospital, Mr. Pottle hadn't been home more than five minutes when there was a knock at his door—and then another—and another.

"Come in. Come in!" he yelled.

The grown-ups stepped in with armfuls of food. The kids stepped in with armfuls of books.

"Thought you could use a little soup."

"And some extra reading while you're laid up."

"Best meatloaf in town."

"Time for us to bring *you* books to read for a change."

The dump man paused, then softly said, "Thank you, everyone."

He sipped some soup, but didn't open any books.

"Go ahead—enjoy the books. Don't mind us."

Another sip, and still Mr. Pottle didn't open any books.

Everyone shifted and glanced at each other.

"Sorry," the kids apologized. "Did we bring you the *wrong* books? We can go get different ones."

Mr. Pottle shushed them. "No, these are perfect. *All* books are perfect. It's just . . . well, I don't know . . . how to read."

The grown-ups coughed uncomfortably and wondered what to say, what to do next.

But the kids knew *exactly* what to do.

"Make room. Move over," they said as they crowded onto the edge of Mr. Pottle's bed. All that day they took turns reading to him—*Where the Wild Things Are*, *Charlotte's Web*, *Alice in Wonderland*.

They couldn't finish all those books in one day, so they returned

day after day, with book after book, reading to Mr. Pottle while he recovered.

After all, it was the least they could do for the dump man, their dump man—who knew how to find treasures in trash.

C is for cat
ALPHABET